Hamish is a Shetland pony who is very proud to be Scottish - so proud that when he is to be sent to England he decides he will be the best pony in the world. But when he gets to London he doesn't understand what anybody is saying, because he only speaks Gaelic. He breaks loose and sets off to see London and so his adventures begin.

Joanna Cannan wrote adult novels and children's books and might be said to have invented the genre of pony books. She wrote A Pony for Jean in 1936 and several other pony books including They Bought Her A Pony and Gaze at the Moon. She was the mother of the Pullein-Thompson sisters who all write pony books. Joanna C

HAMISH

The Story of a Shetland Pony

Joanna Cannan

CAVALIER PAPERBACKS

CAVALIER PAPERBACKS

First published by Puffin Books in 1944

© The Estate of Joanna Cannan

Every effort has been made to trace copyright for the illustrations by Anne Bullen and we apologise for any apparent negligence.

Published by Cavalier Paperbacks 1995

PO Box 1821
Warminster
Wilts BA12 OYD

Cover illustration by Joan Lampkin

ISBN 1-899470-12-3

Typeset by John Leighton Designs
Printed and bound by Cox & Wyman, Reading, Berkshire

CONTENTS

HAMISH

CHAPTER ONE

Hamish was a
little brown
Shetland pony.
He lived in
the West of
Scotland,
between the big dark
hills of the
Highlands and the cold,
green Highland sea.

Hamish was a very proud little pony. He wasn't
proud of his thick brown coat, which kept the
rain out better than any mackintosh. He wasn't
proud of his long brown mane, which kept the
wind off better than any muffler. He wasn't

proud of his bright brown eyes, which could see far away to the furthest islands. He wasn't proud of his little black hoofs, which could gallop without slipping or sliding over rocks and heather. Hamish was only proud of one thing. Like all Scottish people, he was proud of being Scottish.

When Hamish got tired of grazing on the green grass in the strath,* and tired of lying under the birch trees by the brown burn in the glen, he used to climb up a small heathery hillock, from the top of which he could see the strath and the glen and the white sand beaches and the blue islands across the shining strip of sea. He liked it so much that he used to neigh. He neighed, "Scotland for ever!" and the echoes answered him. "Scotland for ever," said the echoes in the big dark hills.

* valley

When Hamish was three years old, his master, whose name was Mr Alexander MacTavish, thought it was time to break him in and sell him for a boy or girl to ride. Mr MacTavish sent some men down to the strath, and they caught Hamish and brought him to a small field near the farm.

Mr MacTavish was a kind man. He didn't expect Hamish to learn everything at once. He taught him to wear a halter first and then a bridle. Then he taught him to wear a saddle and then to carry the shepherd's little boy. When Hamish was  naughty Mr MacTavish scolded him softly in Gaelic, and he always gave him a handful of oats when he was good.

Hamish was often naughty. He tried to be good,
but sometimes, as he walked or trotted round the
dull farm field, he would
suddenly think how much
nicer it had been in the days
when he was a free wild
pony grazing down in the
strath, or lying
by the
burn in
the glen,
or climbing his
heathery little

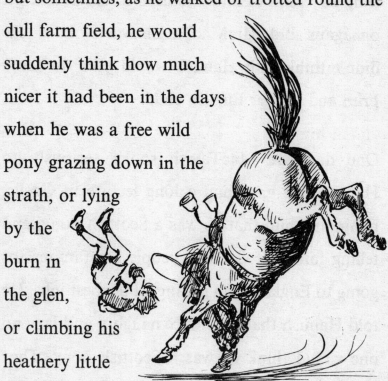

hillock and neighing, "Scotland for ever!" and
being answered by the echoes in the big dark hills.
Then he used to decide to be naughty. Up went
his heels and down went his head, and the
shepherd's little boy shot out of the saddle and

landed on the soft green grass. The shepherd's little boy didn't mind. He used to laugh and get on again. But Mr MacTavish was worried. He didn't think that Hamish would ever do for a prim and proper English child.

One day Mr MacTavish spoke seriously to Hamish. He gave him a long lecture in Gaelic, reminding him that he was a Scottish pony, and telling him that Scottish people are famous for going to England and getting all the best jobs. He told Hamish that if he were naughty and lazy no one would think he was a Scottish pony. They would think he was English or Welsh.

Hamish listened carefully to Mr MacTavish. He thought that at the end of the lecture he might get some oats. He didn't mean to take any notice of the advice that Mr MacTavish was giving him, but when he heard the part about being mistaken for a Welsh or English pony, his pride was stung. He made up his mind that he would be the best pony in the world, so that the glory of Scotland should never grow dim.

From that day onwards Hamish was always good. Mr MacTavish was surprised and pleased.

He wrote out an advertisement and sent it to an English paper. It said, "For sale, a good-looking Shetland pony. Nine hands. Four years. Dog-quiet. Suitable for a Nervous Child."

CHAPTER TWO

Rosemary Ann Worthington was a Nervous Child. If a nice friendly dog ran up to speak to her, she shrieked, "Nanny, will it bite me?" If she saw a fat red cow in a field, she screamed, "Nanny, will it toss me?" If a smart yellow and black striped wasp flew in through the nursery window at tea-time to look for jam she yelled, "Nanny will it sting me?" What Rosemary Ann liked best was to have her hair curled and wear a new dress and be admired.

Rosemary Ann had an Aunt called Aunt Jean. Aunt Jean was both sensible and kind. She thought it would do Rosemary good to have a dog-quiet pony and learn to ride. When she saw the advertisement, which Mr MacTavish had sent to the English newspaper, she wrote to him and asked how much money he wanted for his dog-quiet pony that was suitable for a nervous child. Mr MacTavish wrote back and said that he wanted a hundred pounds. Aunt Jean thought that she could afford a hundred pounds so she sent the money, and said, "Please send the pony as soon as you possibly can."

Mr MacTavish was very pleased to think that Hamish had got a nice home. He told the shepherd's little boy to catch Hamish and ride him to the station and tell the porters to put him in the train. The shepherd's little boy was very sad to think that Hamish was going away so far. He caught him and rode him sorrowfully to the station and bade him a long farewell. When the train stopped at the station the porters put Hamish into a horse box. Hamish was rather frightened. He didn't want to go into the dark horse box. But the porters were kind.

They coaxed him softly in Gaelic and offered him oats and apples and at last he went in. Then the guard blew his whistle and the train, which had been waiting patiently, chugged away. At first Hamish was frightened of the chugging noise, but after a bit he remembered that he was a Scottish pony and that Scottish people are never afraid. So he pretended that he wasn't. He pretended so hard that presently he found that his pretence had come true. Then he ate a bit, and drank a bit and slept a bit, and then he ate a bit more and drank a bit more and slept a bit more. And the evening passed and the night passed and then it was morning, and the train stopped, and people shouted, "Euston Station," and some porters, talking loudly in a strange language, opened the horse box door.

The porters were quite kind men. They looked at Hamish and said, "Hello Pony!" If they had said "Hello Pony!" in Gaelic, Hamish would have understood that they meant to be kind. But Hamish didn't know what "Hello Pony" meant. He could only speak Gaelic. He thought that the porters were wicked horse thieves, who had come to steal him away.

The porters untied the rope headcollar and began to lead him horse box. Hamish tried not to go, but on pulled in front and two porters pushed behind. They pulled and pushed Hamish into a yard, where he was to wait till it was time for him to travel down to Rosemary Ann's home in the country by another train. They tied him to a post and then they went away.

Hamish stood by the post thinking. The yard was dull and dismal and Hamish thought that it was the horse thieves' den.

A Welsh or an English pony might stop there, Hamish thought, but not a Scottish one. He shook his head and then he rubbed it against the post and then he shook it and then he rubbed it again. The headcollar slipped over his little ears and over his little nose, and Hamish gave two little bucks of joy and trotted out of the dull and dismal yard.

Just as Hamish was going out through the gate, the porters came back into the yard. They saw him going, and they shouted, "Oy!" If they had shouted "Oy!" in Gaelic Hamish might have waited for them, but Hamish didn't know what

'Oy!" meant. He could only speak Gaelic. He
turned round and looked at the porters, and they

looked so silly running and shouting that Hamish gave a triumphant neigh. "Scotland for ever!" neighed Hamish and then up went his heels and down went his head and he trotted out into Euston Road.

When Hamish came to some crossroads, a policeman, who had sharp ears and had heard people, shouting "Stop the runaway horse!" was waiting for him. The policeman stretched out his arms and shouted, "Woa." If he had shouted "Woa" in Gaelic, Hamish might have stopped for him, but Hamish didn't understand what "Woa!" meant. He could only speak Gaelic. He stopped for a moment and looked at the policeman and the policeman looked so silly stretching out his arms and shouting that Hamish gave a contemptuous neigh. "Scotland for ever!"

neighed Hamish, and then up went his heels and down went his head and he dodged past the policeman and trotted on down Marylebone Road.

Marylebone Road was full of traffic. A man, who thought he knew all about ponies, saw Hamish coming and stepped off the pavement into the road, holding out his umbrella to stop the traffic. The traffic stopped and the man got ready to stop Hamish. He meant to grab him by his ear or long brown mane. As Hamish came near, the man started saying in a kind voice, "Steady." If he had said "Steady" in Gaelic, Hamish might have slowed down and the man might have caught him. But Hamish didn't know what "Steady" meant. He could only speak Gaelic. He saw that the man meant to catch him, and the man looked so silly wearing a hat and carrying an umbrella and thinking he could catch a Scottish pony, that Hamish gave a scornful neigh, "Scotland for ever!" neighed Hamish, and then up went his heels and down went his head, and he dodged past the man, who grabbed at his mane and only got two hairs, and taking no notice of the traffic lights, which were red and said "Stop," he galloped into Harley Street.

Harley Street wasn't full of traffic; only a few smart and shining cars were rolling along, taking ill people to see the doctors who live there. The ill people in the cars were thinking too much about their aches and pains to bother about Hamish, and though some of the doctors heard the sound of little black hoofs clattering down Harley Street and looked out of their windows, they only said, "Well, well," and went on thinking about mumps and measles. Then, up the street among the smart and shining cars, came an old grey pony dragging a cart that was loaded with vegetables. She was tired and old and very sensible, like all grey ponies. When she saw Hamish galloping down the street, she neighed to him. "I advise you to go home at once," neighed the old grey pony. If she had neighed in Gaelic, Hamish might have stopped for her. But Hamish didn't understand what she meant. He could only speak Gaelic. He stopped for a moment and looked at her, and she looked so silly pulling vegetables and neighing that he neighed back disdainfully. "Scotland for ever!" neighed Hamish, and then up went his heels and down went his head, and he turned left and he turned right and, taking no notice of the traffic lights, which were amber and said nothing, he trotted through Oxford Circus into Regent Street.

Regent Street was full of people shopping. Fat ladies were buying diamonds. Thin ladies were buying furs. Old men were buying motor cars. Young men were buying socks and shoes. Children were buying model railways.

When they heard the sound of Hamish's hoofs, they ran to the shop doors and windows, which shows that a little brown Shetland pony is more exciting than all the diamonds and motor cars and socks and shoes and furs and model railways in Regent Street. "Dear me!" said the fat ladies. "Good gracious!" said the thin ladies. "Tut, tut," said the old men. "By Jove!" said the young men. "Gosh," said the children. But, taking no more notice of them than if they had been seagulls or shellfish, Hamish trotted into Piccadilly Circus.

Piccadilly Circus was full of traffic. It was going
round and round and it made Hamish feel giddy.
He was just going to turn back into Regent Street
when he saw the traffic lights flashing. He
thought that they were the Northern Lights,

which he had often seen flashing across the sky beyond the furthest islands. They made him feel at home, but he was sorry to see that the London people had put them in cages. To keep their courage up and remind them of their native land, he neighed to them. "Scotland for ever!" neighed Hamish, and up went his heels and down went his head and he trotted down Piccadilly.

Hyde Park Corner looked nicer. It was wide and open and beyond some railings was grass and green trees. Hamish was hungry, but he was more thirsty than he was hungry, and the wind which was blowing from his left side, brought the bright shiny smell of water to his nose. He turned towards the smell of water. In front of him was a tall white rock with a hole in it, so Hamish trotted towards the hole, not knowing that the tall white rock was the arch at the top of Constitution Hill and that the hole was the way that only the King or Queen goes through. A Policeman, who was directing the traffic, saw Hamish and was shocked to see a little brown Shetland pony trotting into the hole which only the King or Queen goes through. "You can't go that way!" shouted the policeman. If he had shouted, "You can't go that way!" in Gaelic, Hamish might have gone round, but Hamish didn't know what "You can't go that way!" meant. He could only speak Gaelic. He stopped and looked at the policeman, and the policeman looked so silly directing the traffic and looking shocked that Hamish gave an impudent neigh. "Scotland for ever!" neighed Hamish and the echoes in the arch that only the King or Queen goes through answered him. "Scotland for ever!" said the echoes in the arch that only the King or Queen goes through.

When Hamish came trotting and neighing through the arch, he found himself in Constitution Hill. The bright shiny smell of water was getting stronger and presently Hamish could hear the sound of running water and presently he could see a funny sort of burn. There was a pool in a round white rock, and the water jumped up out of the pool and fell into it again. Hamish thought that it was a spring, but he couldn't understand why the water stayed in the pool and didn't go anywhere. However, he was very thirsty, so he went cautiously up to the funny sort of burn.

The funny sort of burn made a silly pattering noise. It didn't sing songs like the brown burn in the glen. Hamish put his nose in and drank a little. The water was much colder than the brown burn's water and it tasted hard and thin. But it was better than nothing, so, not knowing that he was drinking from the Victoria Memorial fountain outside Buckingham Palace, Hamish drank some more.

While Hamish was drinking from the Victoria Memorial fountain, the third housemaid in Buckingham Palace was dusting a window ledge. She saw the little brown Shetland pony drinking out of the fountain and she told the second housemaid. The second housemaid told the head housemaid and the head housemaid told the third footman and the third footman told the second footman and the second footman told the head footman and the head footman told the Groom of the Chambers and the Groom of the Chambers told the Lady in Waiting and the Lady in Waiting told the Princesses, and they all ran to the windows, which shows that a little brown Shetland pony is more exciting than all the crowns and sceptres and robes and garters in Buckingham Palace.

Hamish drank till he didn't feel thirsty any longer; but he still felt hungry, so he stood by the fountain for a minute with his head up and the wind blowing his mane and his little mouth dripping, while his bright eyes, which could see far away to the furthest islands, looked for some dinner. He looked at Buckingham Palace and at every window there was a head peeping out, and the heads looked so much like little rabbits' heads peeping out of holes in a cliff that Hamish gave a friendly neigh. "Scotland for ever!" neighed Hamish, and then up went his hoofs and down went his head and, noticing the green lawns in St James's Park, he trotted off down Bird Cage Walk to get some dinner.

CHAPTER THREE

In St James's Park a girl called Janet was walking with her governess. It was a very dull walk because the governess, whose name was Miss Pendlebury, would tell Janet the Latin names of the flowers in the borders. Janet liked flowers, but not much. What Janet liked best was animals.

While Miss Pendlebury was telling Janet the Latin name for dandelions, Janet was wishing that she had a pony. Sometimes Janet went to stay with her grandmother, who lived in the country. When she did, her Grandmother used to ask a girl, who lived near, to come to tea and play with her. This girl's name was Rosemary Ann Worthington. The last time that Rosemary Ann had come to tea, she had told Janet that she was going to have a pony. Janet didn't like Rosemary Ann. She thought her a snivelling baby. She was sorry for the pony that was going to belong to Rosemary Ann Worthington.

When Janet had got back to London, she had asked her Daddy to give her a pony. But Janet's Daddy wasn't rich like Mr Worthington. He told Janet that she must save up her pocket money and buy herself a pony.

Janet's pocket money was a pound a week and so far she had five pounds. She knew that a pony cost about a hundred pounds and while Miss Pendlebury was going on about dandelions, Janet was thinking what a long way five pounds was from a hundred pounds.

Suddenly Miss Pendlebury stopped going on about the dandelions. She gave a little scream and said, "Look!" Janet looked. Coming through the gate into St James's Park was a little brown Shetland pony.

Miss Pendlebury knew a lot about flowers. She liked them because they can't bite or kick or scratch or run away, but just stand still and let you pick them. But Miss Pendlebury didn't know anything about ponies. She said, "Look dear, a run-away horse!" and then she said, "Where is the park keeper?"

Janet didn't know much about ponies, but she knew a little, and she could see at once that Hamish was a Shetland pony. Last year Janet's Daddy and Mummy had taken her for a summer holiday to the Highlands of Scotland. A fisherman there had taught Janet some Gaelic. Janet had forgotten most of it, but she still remembered two sentences. They were "Goodnight," and "Scotland for ever!"

While Miss Pendlebury was looking round for the park keeper, Janet walked towards Hamish. She held out her hand and in her hand was one of the lumps of sugar, which she always carried in her pocket in case she should meet a pony. When Hamish saw Janet holding out a lump of sugar he stopped and looked at her. "Goodnight," said Janet in Gaelic.

Hamish was surprised to hear someone saying "Goodnight," in the middle of the morning but he understood that Janet wanted him to stop and talk to her and he thought that perhaps she was just a little absent-minded. He stood quite still and waited for Janet.

Janet walked a little nearer to him. She thought he looked frightened (which was wrong, of course, because Scottish people are never frightened) so she said her other bit of Gaelic. "Scotland for ever!" said Janet, and she looked so nice holding out a lump of sugar and saying "Scotland for ever!" in Gaelic, that Hamish gave a pleased neigh. "Scotland for ever!" neighed Hamish, and then up went his heels and down went his head and he trotted up to Janet.

Janet gave Hamish all the lumps
of sugar in her pocket, and she
patted him and petted
him and said,
"Goodnight"
several times, and
then she
remembered
some more Gaelic.
She remembered,
"Have you caught
a fish?" so she said, '

Have you caught a fish?" to Hamish. Hamish was
surprised to hear someone asking if he had
caught a fish in the middle of London, but he
thought that perhaps Janet was just making
polite conversation. He gave a little snort and

looked in Janet's pockets for some more sugar.

While Hamish and Janet were talking Gaelic, Miss Pendlebury had found the Park Keeper. His name was Mr Mink and he knew Janet. He had often told her to keep off the grass. He came up and said in a cross voice, "Run along, Miss. I'll take charge of that there runaway pony." If he had said, "I'll take charge of that there runaway pony in Gaelic, Hamish might have gone on looking for sugar in Janet's pockets and Mr Mink might have taken charge of him, but Hamish didn't know what "I'll take charge of that there runaway pony" meant. He could only speak Gaelic. He stopped looking for sugar and looked at Mr Mink, and Mr Mink looked so silly walking along and talking in a cross voice that Hamish gave a mocking neigh. "Scotland for ever!" neighed Hamish, and then up went his heels and down went his head and Mr Mink found himself sitting in the middle of a flower bed on the top of his best Begonias.

Miss Pendlebury screamed. Janet laughed. Mr Mink rose up from his squashed Begonias. He saw that Janet was still holding on to Hamish, so he said, "You'd better hold him, Miss, while I telephone for a policeman."

He went away to telephone and Janet petted Hamish and patted him and said "Goodnight" and, "Scotland for ever!" and "Have you caught a fish?" in Gaelic.

Presently the policeman came. He had brought a lot more policemen and a horse box, all for Hamish. The porters at Euston Station had told the police that they had lost a pony addressed to Miss Rosemary Ann Worthington, and the horse box was going to take Hamish straight down to Rosemary Ann's home in the country.

Mr Mink was very silly.
He got a thick stick
and began to say
"Shoo!" to Hamish.
But the policemen
were much more sensible.
They asked Janet to
coax Hamish into the horse box.
Janet put her arm round Hamish's neck and said
"Goodnight," and, "Scotland for ever!" and

"Have you caught a fish?" and walked slowly towards the horse box. Hamish went with her. They walked up the ramp of the horse box talking Gaelic together. Then Janet slipped out, and the policemen shut the door of the horse box and told the driver to drive on to Rosemary Ann's home in the country.

When the horse box had gone and the policemen had gone and Mr Mink had gone, Miss Pendlebury began to tell Janet the Latin name for daisies. Janet began to swallow, and then she began to sniff, and then she began to cry - it was so dull without Hamish. Miss Pendlebury said that Janet couldn't cry in St James's Park, but Janet did. She cried until she remembered not to be like Rosemary Ann Worthington.

CHAPTER FOUR

When Hamish arrived at Rosemary Ann's home in the country, he was put into a meadow with plenty of grass in it, and trees for shade, and a nice big trough full of water. Hamish was pleased. He remembered what Mr MacTavish had said about Scottish people coming to England and getting all the best jobs. He thought that he had got one of the best jobs and he made up his mind to be a very good pony.

Rosemary Ann wasn't very excited about Hamish. She didn't come out and look at him for ages. When she did, she was dressed up in smart new riding clothes. Her Mummy and her Nanny and the gardener, whose name was Mr Potts came with her.

Mr Potts caught Hamish and saddled and bridled him and Hamish was very good and stood as still as a statue. Then Rosemary Ann's Nanny lifted Rosemary Ann into the saddle. While Rosemary Ann had been dressing up in her smart new riding clothes she had wanted to ride Hamish, but as soon as she was on his back she began to feel nervous. "He's going to kick! I shall fall off! Nanny, Nanny, lift me down," screamed Rosemary Ann Worthington.

Rosemary Ann's Nanny was
quite sensible. She said
"Nonsense," and,
"Don't be silly."
But Rosemary Ann
still screamed. She
screamed and screamed and
then she got into a rage.
She kicked and waved her
smart new riding stick.

Hamish had been frightened
by Rosemary Ann's screaming.
If she had screamed in Gaelic, he might have
helped her off by bucking, but Hamish didn't
know what her screaming meant. He could only
speak Gaelic. He thought it was best to stand
quite still and pretend he wasn't afraid till his

pretence came true. But when Rosemary Ann kicked his ribs hard and waved her riding stick, he thought that she wanted him to set off at a fast gallop. He jumped forward, jerking the reins out of Mr Pott's hand, and to please Rosemary he galloped as fast as he could to the other side of the meadow. He was too busy galloping to notice that Rosemary Ann wasn't on his back any more.

When Hamish got to the other side of the meadow, he began to wonder which way Rosemary Ann wanted him to go now. He stopped and then he noticed that she wasn't

there, so he started eating. Presently Mr Potts
came up to him
and took off
his saddle and
bridle. Hamish
thought that was
rather silly. He
knew that Rosemary

Ann had fallen off, but he had expected her to
laugh and get on again.

When Rosemary Ann had fallen off, she hadn't
hurt herself a bit. She was just frightened and
cross. She cried for ages and said that she never
wanted to ride again. She said she hated ponies.
So her mother telephoned to Aunt Jean and said
that it was no good giving Rosemary Ann a pony.
Aunt Jean was rather annoyed. She said, "Next
time I have to give Rosemary Ann a present I

shall give her sewing things." Of course Hamish was much too small for Aunt Jean to ride herself, so at first she thought she would sell him. Then she thought of all the boys and girls who would like a pony, but haven't enough money to buy one. She remembered someone telling her about a girl who was saving up to buy a pony, and she remembered that the girl's grandmother lived near Rosemary Ann and that the girl's name was Janet. Aunt Jean wrote to Janet's grandmother and said that she would like to give a good-looking dog-quiet Shetland pony to Janet.

Janet's Grandmother was old but nice. She wrote back and said, "Thank you very much,"and that the pony could live in her orchard and belong to Janet. She didn't tell Janet, but the next time that Janet came to stay (which was quite soon) she said, "There is a present for you in the orchard."

Janet thought that perhaps the present was a duck or a hen or even a tame goose. She went to the orchard gate and looked over and there was her old friend Hamish.

When Janet saw Hamish she thought that she must be dreaming, but she pinched herself and she felt the pinch, so she knew that she was awake. She climbed over the orchard gate and then she stopped and looked at Hamish and he looked so lovely with the wind blowing his long brown mane about and his bright brown eyes, which could see far away to the furthest islands, looking at her, that she called to him. "Scotland for ever!" called Janet and she went running across the orchard to Hamish.

Hamish had been eating grass. He heard someone climbing the orchard gate, so he stopped eating and looked up and saw Janet and she looked so nice running across the orchard and calling that Hamish gave a happy neigh. "Scotland for ever!" neighed Hamish, and then up went his heels and down went his head and he trotted across the orchard to Janet.

THEY BOUGHT HER A PONY
BY JOANNA CANNAN

Angela Peabody has the bad luck to be the only child of rich and doting parents. They consider her 'a grand little horsewoman,' and when they go to live in the country, buy her an expensive pony and expect that the local people will get a surprise when they see her flying over jumps. However, Angela is not quite such a good rider as they imagine.

Angela soon meets a local family of six children who share three ponies and this books tells of Angela's mistakes and her adventures and of the triumphs and disasters for all the children at the local gymkhana.

NEW FROM THE PULLEIN-THOMPSON SISTERS

HORSEHAVEN

BY CHIRSTINE PULLEIN-THOMPSON

This is the story of a group of children wo are determined to save their local Riding Stables from financial ruin. Their dreams come true when they turn the stables into a Horse and Pony Sanctuary, raising funds to make it work. They rescue ponies which have been terribly neglected and are on the point of death, but are devastated when they finally find out what happened to Fantasy whom they thought they had found a good home.

THE LONG RIDE HOME
BY DIANA PULLEIN-THOMPSON

The story is set on a tiny Scottish island and the land through which its fourteen year old heroine, Carey rides to her Grandmother's Yorkshire cottage. In the summer holidays Carey, is left on the island with her dog Tina and pony Sandpiper, while her parents travel the world. Carey is left in the charge of her half-sister Hannah who turns out to be an imposter, although Carey doesn't realise it at the time. Carey feels that she is a prisoner in her own home and resolves to leave.

RACE HORSE HOLIDAY
BY JOSEPHINE PULLEIN-THOMPSON

Race Horse Holiday tells the story of Vivien and Jon who spend three weeks at a Racing Stables and get involved in the exciting mystery of a horse that may have been doped and the new apprentice who goes missing.